JAMES STEVENSON

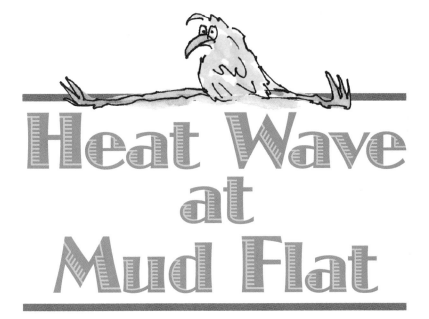

Heat Wave at Mud Flat

GREENWILLOW BOOKS, NEW YORK

For Susan —
a hundred times over

Copyright © 1997 by James Stevenson
Watercolor paints and a black pen were used for the full-color art.
The text type is Cochin BT.

Printed in Singapore by Tien Wah Press
First Edition 10 9 8 7 6 5 4 3

Library of Congress Cataloging-in-Publication Data

Stevenson, James, (date)
Heat wave at Mud Flat / by James Stevenson.
p.   cm.
Summary: The animals of Mud Flat pay Raymond the Rainmaker to bring
relief from the hot weather, but even though he fails, rain finally comes.
ISBN 0-688-14205-2 (trade).   ISBN 0-688-14206-0 (lib. bdg.)
[1. Rain and rainfall—Fiction.   2. Weather—Fiction.
3. Animals—Fiction.]   I. Title   PZ7.S84748Hc   1997
[E]—dc20   95-5462   CIP   AC

Contents

1
Hot

It was boiling hot in Mud Flat. There was
no breeze, and it hadn't rained in months.

"This is the hottest
I have ever been,"
said George.
"My fur is soaked.
I squish when I walk."

"You call that hot?"
said Alex. "I can't even
hop to the river
and take a dip."

"My legs have turned   to spaghetti,"
said Eleanor.

"When I try to make my cricket noises,"
said Orkney, "nobody hears them.
I sound like wet feathers."

"We slide right off rocks," said Janet.
"Can't get a grip," said Elwood.
"Too slippery," said Maurice.

"I'd fly to some cooler place," said Duper.
"But I just can't get off the ground."

"Moss is growing inside my shell,"
  said Warfield. "It's a jungle in there."

"You know what I dream about?"
  said Laurie. "Rain. Spattering, splattering,
  plipping, plopping, gurgling, glopping rain."
"I hope it comes soon," said Kenneth.
"I'm turning to dust before
  my very eyes."

2
The Blizzard

3

Shadows

Philip the snail sat in the shadow
of Otis the mouse.
Otis sat in the shadow of
Rudolph the rabbit.
Rudolph sat in the shadow
of Diane the pig.
Diane lay in the shadow
of Diego the bear.
Diego stood in the shadow
of Katrina the hippo.
Katrina stood in the shadow
of Marty the elephant.

"Out of the sun at last," said Philip the snail.

"This is nice and shady," said Otis.

"I feel cool," said Rudolph.

"I'm glad to be out of the sun," said Diane.

"You said it," said Diego.

"What a relief,"
 said Katrina.

"This is good for all of you," said Marty.

"But I'm HOT!"
 Katrina said, "I'm sorry, Marty."
 Diego said, "I wish we could help."
 Diane said, "I do, too."

Rudolph said, "Any ideas?"

Otis said, "Not me."

Philip said, "I have one."

Philip whispered to Otis.

Otis whispered to Rudolph.

Rudolph whispered to Diane.

Diane whispered to Diego.

Diego whispered to Katrina.

Katrina said, "Good idea!"

"Thank you, Marty," said Philip. "Now
it's our turn!"
Rudolph and Otis shaded Marty's trunk.
Diane shaded Marty's ears.
Diego shaded Marty's face.
Katrina shaded Marty's body.
Philip shaded Marty's tail.

"How do you feel, Marty?" said Philip.
"Cool, thank you," said Marty. "Nice
and cool."

4

The Big Snowstorm

YOU WERE AROUND FOR THE GREAT SNOWSTORM OF 1925, WEREN'T YOU, MR. GIDDINGS?

INDEED I WAS.

COULD YOU TELL US ABOUT IT?

IT WAS BITTER COLD. IT SNOWED FOR TWO WEEKS. EVERYTHING TURNED TO ICE. ALL YOU COULD DO WAS SHIVER. THE WIND HOWLED. THEN THE SNOW TURNED TO SLEET, AND IT GOT EVEN COLDER....

OH, IT WAS A TERRIBLE STORM....

I KNEW THAT WOULD COOL US OFF.

I FEEL QUITE REFRESHED.

5

The Mirage

"Did you ever see a mirage?" said Chumley.
"I don't know," said Walt. "What is it?"

"It's when it's very, very hot, and you think
you see something," said Chumley, "but
there's nothing there."

"Such as what?" said Walt.

"Such as a castle, or somebody
on a horse," said
Chumley. "Anything."

"I think I see a mirage right now,"
said Walt.

"It's pretty soon for a mirage," said
Chumley, "since I just this minute told
you what it was."

"It's a mirage, all right," said Walt. "Right
over there."

"What do you see?" said Chumley. "I don't
see a thing."

"I see a river and a castle with flags and
soldiers and two hundred horses, some
with stripes."

"Horses don't have stripes," said Chumley.
"It's my mirage," said Walt. "They have
stripes."

"You know what I see?" said Chumley.

"What?" said Walt.

"I see a dopey skunk."

"That's not a very fancy mirage," said Walt.

"I didn't *say* it was a mirage," said Chumley.

6
Ice Cream

IT'S HARDLY WORTH GETTING ICE CREAM IN THIS WEATHER.

ALL IT DOES IS MELT.

YOU'RE WASTING YOUR TIME, CHESTER.

7

Raymond
the Rainmaker

"This heat is terrible," said Harold.

"What we need is rain," said Alex. "A lot of rain."

"Did somebody say 'rain'?" said a voice. It was a
green lizard. He was carrying a suitcase. "I am
Raymond the Rainmaker."

"You make rain?" said Alex.

"You know how to do that?" said Harold.
The lizard put down his suitcase.

"Raymond the Rainmaker will amaze you,"
he said. He began unpacking umbrellas.

"What are the umbrellas for?" said Harold.

"To keep you dry, of course," said Raymond
the Rainmaker. "Who wants an umbrella?
Only 25 cents—and they're guaranteed for
the heaviest downpour."

"He must know what he's doing,"
said Harold.
Harold and Alex bought umbrellas.

Pretty soon a crowd gathered. They all
bought umbrellas.

Raymond the Rainmaker started mixing
things in a mixing bowl.

"What's he doing?" said Eleanor.
"Getting ready to make rain," said Leo.
"Thank goodness," said Eleanor.
"Everybody ready to be amazed?" said
  Raymond.
"Yes!" yelled the crowd. "Yes!"

"This will require an additional 25 cents,"
said Raymond. He went around with his
open suitcase. Everybody dropped a
quarter into it.

"Here we go!" said Raymond.

There was a flash and a boom, and
a big cloud of green smoke.

When the smoke floated away, Raymond
the Rainmaker was gone. So were his
suitcase and his mixing bowl.
"Amazing," said Harold.
"Amazing," said Alex.

Everybody looked at the sky. It was
sunny and clear.

"I don't see any rain," said Diane.

"Or even any rain clouds," said Katrina.

"I guess we keep the umbrellas," said
Chumley.

"Might as well," said Mr. Giddings. "They
help keep the sun off."

After a while they all took their umbrellas
and went home.

8
Good Deed

9
Rain

Just when nobody thought it would ever
happen, rain came. It poured all day long,
soaking Mud Flat from one end to the
other.

In the evening they all put their umbrellas
together and had a party underneath them.
They ate damp cookies and talked about
how hot it used to be.
And when Raymond the Rainmaker
turned up, asking for more money because
of the rain, nobody minded. They just gave
him a cookie.